AWAKE

AWAKE

nancy johnson

Minerva Rising Press
Boca Raton

ISBN 978-1-950811-12-0

Cover photo by Adam Niescioruk
Book design by Brooke Schultz

Printed and bound in USA
First Printing November 2021

Published by Minerva Rising Press
17717 Circle Pond Ct
Boca Raton, FL 33496
www.minervarising.com

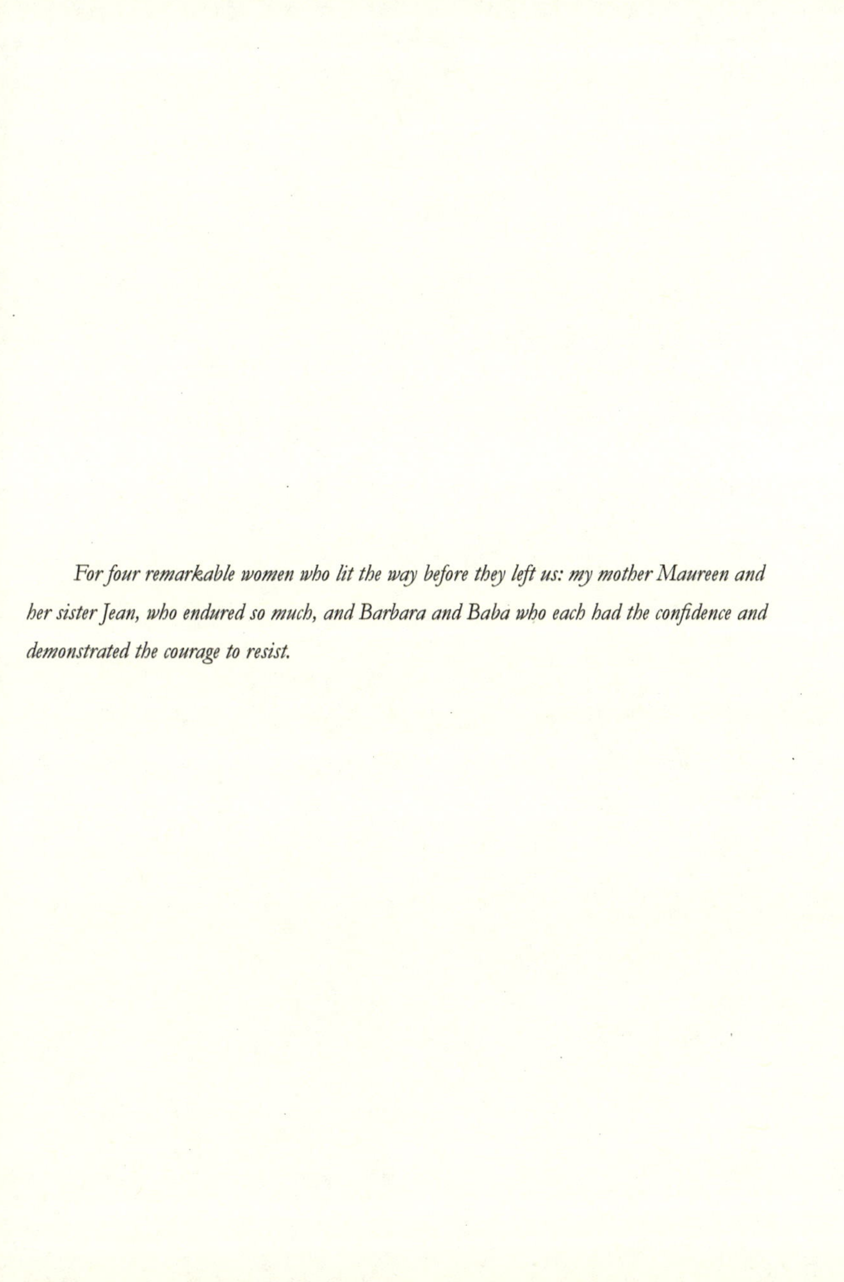

For four remarkable women who lit the way before they left us: my mother Maureen and her sister Jean, who endured so much, and Barbara and Baba who each had the confidence and demonstrated the courage to resist.

This is *my* life, Doctor."

The young man inches from me in my room at Forest Home is my daughter's age. Both go to the same gym, travel the same circles.

A faint, antiseptic whiff tickles my nostrils as his small hands pull the stethoscope from his ears, unwrap the blood pressure cuff. He looks into my eyes. So stern, like that pious priest spewing fire and brimstone when we were children. I was only eight when Mama's last baby was stillborn. I never heard what the priest said, but Mama was slumped in her chair, heaving deep sobs by the time Daddy walked in. Without a word, Daddy gripped the back of the little man's starched collar, practically lifted him off his feet, and steered him clear across the living room floor. And that wasn't the last time the door slammed behind a preacher. They would come, but Daddy told them all the same thing—he wouldn't go back to church until God did.

"Now, Frances."

I've never used that tone on my elders. I arch my eyebrow, but he carries on.

"I said not to change anything. Side effects are inevitable." He wags his manicured finger in my face. I clamp my jaw.

A slight breeze rustles the lace curtains beside me. I gaze out through them. A hummingbird flits at the feeder on the oak branch stretching past my window.

"I feel more alive than I have in years."

He gestures toward my bony hand. "The tremor is back."

"So?" Like everyone else, I'd been a willing consumer of quick-fix pills to fend off symptoms of aging. But they worked too well. At one time, I knew my body, its rhythms and patterns. Then I lost all contact with signs and signals that used to guide me. So, a month ago, I stopped everything. Cold turkey. The effect was almost instant; reminded me of those first gasps of air when I'd break surface after diving too deep at the swimming hole.

"Doctor, I think of this shaky hand as heralding my body's release from chemical bondage."

He sniffs, stands, wheels my claw-foot piano stool back under the antique desk. "If you feel that way, you should find another physician."

I loathe conflict. But since I stopped the daily smorgasbord of capsules and tablets, my stomach grumbles, joints ache, I pass gas, and I even look forward to my hand vibrating at a steady pace. Like that hummingbird's wings. Those little creatures may have short lives, but the lives they have are vibrant.

"It's not personal. I haven't been feeling right, so I researched on the Internet." My trembling right hand points toward my computer. "And figured out I was taking too many drugs. This is *my* body. My decision. I wish you would respect that."

"The almighty Internet. One or two layman's articles and everyone's an expert. I don't suppose they were based on randomized controlled trials?" He turns away and says under his breath, "Probably never heard of an RCT. Dr. Oprah, I expect."

"Do you speak to your mother like that?" I grasp the arms of my easy chair and sit forward. "You forget I am one of the few residents here with perfect hearing. And for your personal edification, I have a Ph.D. in microbiology. There is another doctor in this room, one old enough to know there is more to the practice of medicine than scientific experiments. As for finding another physician, unless one of us leaves here, which I am not likely to do alive, then I'm afraid we are quite stuck with each other."

"I'm not so sure." He gathers his things without so much as a glance in my direction.

"Well, I would hate to bother the courts to convince you." Amazing, really, how the word "court" commands attention.

I suck in a long breath and press on. "But my daughter is quite prepared for any lawsuit. You know, young man, you would be well advised to remember that just because we grow old, does not mean we automatically grow stupid."

He stares down at me like my husband did that last time. It was the first time I thought he might hit me, and the last time I ever saw him.

A long silence. He blinks. "There's no point in regular checkups if you won't follow my advice. Honestly, your behaviour makes me question your competence. I'll have to talk to administration about what to do with you. In the meantime, if you have anything urgent, let the nurse know. Is that satisfactory," he pauses, "Doctor?"

"Fine, thank you, Doctor."

He snatches his little black bag from the bed and walks off with his head bent, texting something to God knows who. When the door closes behind him, my posture slackens and I'm inches smaller. A hollow chill creeps into my stomach. What have I done?

I stand before my antique mirror contemplating possible eviction. On the inside, it's like the last sixty years never happened. I'm that same girl who chewed my nails in front of the principal's office while awaiting sentencing for almost neutering the class bully with my knee. But there's no escaping that the last six decades happened to the image staring back from the glass. A late-life Katherine Hepburn springs to mind, same frame, same nest of hair, same shake. "Life is hard," she once said. "After all, it kills you." I lean forward, grip both sides of the dresser and glare at myself. *Time's wasting, Frances. Do you really want to spend what's left cowering in your room?*

I open the door to a steady stream of traffic in the hallway. It's mid-afternoon, only forty-eight hours since death finished taunting the last tenant, but already the paint is dry and a new victim is in the vacant room down the hall. It's a fact of our lives we come here to die and many actually yearn to meet their maker. But death doesn't take reservations, and until *it* is ready for *us*, we wait more and less patiently here at Forest Home.

I reach down, flip open the paisley box of note cards I keep as volunteer greeter. I sign one and pick up the yellow sweetheart roses from the gift shop.

Movers carry more loads past my door. So much stuff. How will it all fit? I look around my own compact quarters and sigh. My spacious life condensed to a bed, a chair, a desk, a dresser.

The once ample contents of my walk-in closet collapsed to fit the narrow armoire in the corner.

The bustle stops, and I head down the hall. My rickety right hand delivers five woodpecker raps to the partially closed door. "Hello," I call into the opening, "Welcome Wagon."

A broad face with dark, sparkling eyes appears from behind the door.

"Well aren't you neighborly," the smiling woman, who smells faintly of gingerbread, says. "I just got here this morning and here you are already. Come in, girl." Her hair is salt with only a sprinkle of pepper, cropped short and blunt, framing her round face in a pageboy that brings me back to the schoolyard of my youth.

"I'm Frances." I extend my tremorous hand, and she grasps it in both of hers.

"Mabel, of Willy and Mabel." She points to the painting above the double bed. "My Willy gave me that on our fiftieth. He says it couldn't be more like us than if we posed for the artist ourselves. It's called, 'Tango.'"

The canvas is mounded with fleshy characters splashed in rich, primary colours. A chubby, bald senior gazes adoringly down at his plump partner who he holds in a low dip on the dance floor.

She accepts the basket of flowers and is bent over, placing them on the window ledge when a deep baritone calls from the doorway. "I'd know that breathtaking backside anywhere. How's life, Mabel?"

We turn at the same time to face a door full of lanky denim. Mabel laughs. "Well, I'll be damned. Morley O'Brien. What's it been, ten years?"

"Funny how it feels like yesterday," he says as they part from a warm embrace. "How long since me and Willy pulled your braids in history class?"

She chuckles. "I'm brand new here. Do you know Frances? The Welcome Wagon lady? We just met."

"Nope. Haven't had the pleasure. Only moved in myself a few days ago. When's the Welcome Wagon lady knockin' on *my* door?" He looks down at me with Paul Newman eyes, and I hope they can't see me shiver.

"I just greet women who move in," I answer.

"Sounds like my kind of job. Let me know when you get tired of it and I'll take over for you, Frances," he says, and Mabel laughs.

He finally stops looking at me and gestures to the "Tango" canvas over the bed. "You and Willy pose for that thing?"

Mabel slaps his arm and turns to me. "See? Just like I told you, Frances. Willy said that picture is us."

Morley laughs and points to the old recliner in front of the TV. "Willy still has that old thing? Where is he anyway? Every morning I read the obits and haven't seen me or Willy yet. Figured he was still with you."

"He's in Starlight Wing, where they need more care. Been there a month." The light leaves her eyes and her tone is low. "I'm alone, kids scattered across the country. We've both had pretty serious health problems, and the plan was for me and Willy to get a room together when a double's available. But Willy got sick, went downhill so quickly he had to get admitted. The commute every day was killing me, so, when a single opened this week, I took it. We just spent a fortune on new adjustable hospital beds that we can put together as a double. They let me squeeze them in here. A little cramped but now I don't have to travel while we wait to be together." She looks up at Morley and frowns. "Maybe it's my imagination, but since he's been here he seems to be getting worse."

We're all getting worse, I think, and my mind sinks back to my encounter with the doctor. But before I can descend further, Mabel flashes a fresh smile at Morley and lifts me back to the present. "So, old friend, what's a nice guy like you doing in a rockin' place like this?"

Something buzzes on his hip and he lifts a cell phone to his ear, waves to us and walks away. "Don't want to interrupt your unpackin'. Catch up over rummy after dinner?"

"Best offer I've had in years. We'll be there." She turns to me. "Right, Frances?"

It's seven in the evening and we're the only residents still up in the Sunshine Wing dining room. Our table looks out through a floor-to-ceiling window into the dimming autumn woods. Mabel is on my left, Morley's on my right, and the scent of turkey dinner still hangs in the air.

Mabel's pudgy fingers finish the deal and turn up the last card on the oak tabletop. "You have some nerve, girl." She chuckles and gives me a look of admiration that makes me squirm. "Good thing your daughter's a lawyer. I didn't know you could sue for being dropped as a patient."

I clear my throat as Morley's big mitt discards the nine of clubs. "Actually, I'm not certain you can." Now they both look at me with wide eyes. I shift in my seat, my tremor speeds up. "He took me by surprise. I didn't expect him to be so hostile." My restless fingers pick up Morley's discarded nine, retrieve five more clubs from my hand, line them up on the table in front of me and snap my last card face up. "I'm out."

"Well, I hope by that you only mean this card game," Morley laughs, and I grimace. Sensitivity doesn't appear to be his strong suit.

He tilts back in his chair. I've always been attracted to a thick head of hair on a man, and though silver, his is full and wavy and makes him look closer to sixty than the seventy-eight years Mabel said he is. I can't believe he's ogling me, staring at my chest. Everything about him reminds me of high school.

"You're quite a gal."

Mabel giggles. "I've known this old rascal since grade school, and he hasn't changed a darn bit. Watch out for him, Frances."

"Or what, I'll get her pregnant?" He grins with teeth that look too perfect to be real.

I've never kissed a mouth full of dentures. In fact, it's been decades since I've kissed a mouth full of anything, and I can't believe I'm actually thinking about this.

Mabel slaps at his firm bicep and the plump folds under her thin, knit top jiggle as she laughs. "Still a lech, but a charming old lech. So, old friend, where have you been most of my life?"

"When Gert died, the place got kinda messy. The girls figured it was because I was senile or something."

"Don't they know what a slob you are?" Mabel rolls her eyes.

"Guess not. Gert always took care of that stuff, and I was away a lot when they were kids. The life of a construction worker." He shrugs. "Anyway, I moved in with the oldest. She set up her little basement apartment for me. I don't know what they expected. I'm a grown man with needs if you catch my drift."

"Ha! As I recall, your *needs* started long before you were all grown." Mabel giggles.

"Yeah, well, they caught me with women a couple of times. Young stuff."

I cringe. I haven't heard that term since everyone snickered when my husband walked out with a girl half his age. He left me with two adolescents, emptied the bank accounts, and trashed my self-esteem.

Morley sees my reaction. "C'mon, Frances. They were just ten years younger. About your age."

Mabel laughs. "Never thought I'd live long enough to consider seventy-year-olds young stuff. So, what happened?"

"Well, my girls talked to the doctor and together they decided it was all symptoms of raging dementia. So here I am."

I look at him as he deals the hand. "Some scientific evaluation of dementia. Why didn't you fight that?"

"You are a scrapper, aren't you?" he says, and I wince. *Maybe I do challenge things too much. Maybe…*

"Anyway," Morley continues, "why bother? Here someone takes care of me, I'm with people my own age who don't judge me, and besides, I heard the ratio of girls to guys here was ten to one. What's to fight?"

He stares into my eyes long enough to ignite my cheeks and I feel like a silly schoolgirl. Hormones? At my age? I look down, retrieve my cards and fan them in front of my face like a shy girl in an Austen scene.

"But I must admit, I thought it would be livelier. Been here almost two weeks already and haven't heard one note of music. What gives with these people? Course it could be this blasted thing is busted." He wiggles the tiny beige bud in his left ear.

"It's not your hearing aid," I say. Everything was bright and airy with energy in the air when Forest Home, brand new and nestled in hardwoods at the town's edge, opened. The community was abuzz about this state-of-the art facility, modern yet homey. Back then the place hummed with bingo, cards, visitors and music. But it seemed only a matter of weeks before the clouds descended on Sunshine Wing. "They say they don't have enough staff for activities."

"Yeah, right," he says. "I'm not talking about staff. There's no life in the residents. If you ask me, it's the meds. Glad to hear you tossed yours. I never take anything myself unless it has hops or grapes or can be mixed with Pepsi. I flush their little pills down the toilet when they're not looking. Keeps everyone happy."

I think back to the beginning when every meal was preceded by people talking and smiling in animated walker and wheelchair races to the dining room. When was that replaced by the slow herd of shuffling feet and frozen stares? I remember my own sluggish existence on prescription drugs when I spent hours alone in my room. "I'm beginning to think you have a point."

Mabel retrieves a card from the deck. "C'mon, you two. If it wasn't for modern medicine we wouldn't be here."

Morley and I exchange looks and shake our heads. "Mabel, my love," he touches her hand, "you inspire me. It's nice to know that human goodness can survive almost eight decades of life's battering ram. But haven't you learned the difference between God and a doctor?"

Mabel shakes her head.

"God doesn't think he's a doctor," Morley says.

"Be still my heart. Where have you been all my life?" I say aloud before I can catch myself.

Morley ripples with laughter, and I don't know if I'm laughing harder at him or his joke, but we lose track of the hand, give up and toss our cards in the middle of the table.

Mabel's face turns serious. "C'mon, Morley. You know my nephew, George's boy, the doctor. It's not easy. No staff, long hours, everyone watching them, the threat of lawsuits."

"Sounds like my life as a crane operator on high-rise construction," Morley says.

"But they make life and death decisions," Mabel says.

"Like controlling a steel girder from fifteen floors up?"

"Be serious, Morley. They have some real problems."

He shakes his head.

"What?" Mabel asks.

"Isn't he the one with the six-figure income, the big house, takes the family on fancy trips all the time?"

"What if he does? He earned all that."

"And isn't he the one who was having trouble deciding whether to give his twins new BMW convertibles for their sixteenth birthdays because he was afraid that would look too uppity?"

"What's your point?"

"Some people have all the good problems, don't you think?" He winks at me, and Mabel reaches out to slap him just as the lights flicker. We look over to the personal support worker at the nurses' desk. Jenny, a diminutive brunette, smiles back and points to her watch. It's time to get to our rooms.

"Yeah, now you mention it, Morley," Mabel pushes her chair under the table, "I'd trade problems with my nephew. After five decades of sharing it, my bed feels pretty empty these days. I'm losing hope I'll ever get my old dancing partner back. But I'm not so sure going against a doctor is the answer. Then what would happen when you really need one?"

I try hard to banish that thought from my mind as Morley shakes his head and swaggers down one hallway while Mabel and

I head to our rooms in the opposite direction. But before we part she stops, looks at me with genuine concern and rekindles my fear. "You have a pretty serious condition, Frances. Aren't you nervous you won't get help when you need it?"

I lie in bed and try hard to summon sleep. But my mind won't shut down. The system seems to be working against Mabel's marriage and Morley shouldn't even be here. And what about me? My kids are nearby but busy. Successful professionals, they live life just as I taught them. Their "problems" remind me of the sort I once had—they need to find time for their dutiful weekly calls or manage to actually visit on special occasions. Today, I threatened that young doctor with a daughter I haven't seen in weeks and who has no real clue about my condition. What on earth have I done? The only physician for this home thinks I'm crazy, wants me evicted. I turn on my side, stare into the darkness and feel certain of one thing. All the *good* problems, if we ever had any, are a thing of the past for everyone here at Forest Home.

A week passes with no word from the doctor, the administrator, no white coats coming to take me away. I should just be relieved, but it's mid-morning, and I'm at my computer again, searching other nursing home sites, just in case. I feel a presence at my door and turn. Mabel is standing there, her face ashen, her forehead pinched in a painful-looking frown. "What's wrong?" I put my arm around her shoulders and guide her to sit on my bed. I stroke my hand up and down her back. She stares straight ahead, her eyes wide and fearful, her whole body trembling.

After several moments she turns slowly, faces me with blank

eyes and I shudder. In a low monotone she says, "I just saw Willy. He looked at me and said, 'You remind me so much of my wife, Mabel.'" A pause. Then in half breath and half voice she says, "Willy. Doesn't. Know me."

Sobs as forceful as physical assaults wrack Mabel's body. Two nurses appear, a young male and a harried-looking middle-aged woman.

"C'mon, Mabel," the young fellow says, "the doctor can give you something to calm your nerves."

As they wheel her away she wails, "It's not me that needs help. Can't he give Willy something to bring him back?"

"I heard they discharged Mabel from the hospital. Have you seen her yet?" Morley sits across from me as we wait for lunch to be served.

"No, and I'm worried. It's been ten days."

"God, have you seen Willy?" he asks.

I shake my head. I'd only known Mabel for a week before this turn of events, and never met Willy.

Morley straightens the napkin on his lap. "Poor bastard. Lying in bed. All rigid and bent in a fetal position. The Willy I knew was plump and jolly. Like Mabel. They sure did like their food." He shakes his head. "Now his legs are like friggin' toothpicks. His body twitches and he just stares. Doesn't even know I'm there. Poor bastard."

"No wonder they medicated her. That would be tough to deal with."

"Right. Just what she needs, a friggin' pill. C'mon Frances,

I can't believe you of all people just said that. Are you friggin' blind?"

"Oh Morley, even I know medicine has its place. You didn't see her."

"Yeah," he nods his head over my left shoulder. "So, this is better?"

I turn to look. Mabel shuffles into the dining room, part of that growing herd of glassy-eyed zombies who seem to be everywhere now. Morley helps her into her seat and my heart squeezes as she looks right through me. She doesn't even smell like Mabel, the usual mix of Ivory soap and cinnamon replaced by sour urine and age. We eat in silence. I wipe some drool from Mabel's chin and cut the chicken strips on her plate. Morley and I take turns guiding the fork to her mouth. I try with my shaky hand, but in the end he gets more accomplished.

He reaches across the table, gently grabs my wrist and speaks in a low tone. "Jenny told me they're looking for a bed for her in Starlight Wing. Some jackass decided she has rapid onset dementia." His jaw is tense and his teeth clamped tight, so I'm caught off guard when he starts to smile—a manic, crazy smile. He releases my arm and sits back. "Willy and Mabel will be together after all. They won't know each other, but at least they'll be together." He laughs.

Tears sting my eyes. I look at Mabel, oblivious to everything he said. I throw my napkin on the table and turn to Morley. "There is nothing funny about any of this."

"I know, Frances. You can cry. But a man has to laugh, or yell or hit something. In the end it's all the same thing."

He takes my napkin and dabs at a tear sliding from the corner of my eye. "Anyway, I have a plan." He grins. This time it's that heart-melting, boyish grin of his. "Trust me," he says, and I can't believe what I'm feeling. I'm too old to learn how to trust again, especially a man, let alone one like him. I know his wanton ways. A "charming old lech" Mabel called him. So why am I melting under his gaze?

Lunch is over. None of the three of us has eaten much, but Morley doesn't seem to notice. "You take her back to her room. I'll meet you there. No matter what anyone suggests when I get there, just agree, okay?"

What choice do I have? I needed to be strong for me and the kids, but I'm so tired of facing things alone. Now here's a man with a plan. I haven't met one of those in decades. "Whatever you say," I answer in a quiet voice.

"Good girl." He smiles down on me, pats Mabel's shoulder and heads toward the nursing station.

I watch for a moment. Soon he and the nurses laugh and I'm angry. What kind of plan involves flirting with a bunch of nurses? Men!

In Mabel's catatonic state, I could be anyone or anything. I guide her like a puppeteer, back to her room, and into Willy's easy chair in front of the television. I remember she likes *Days of Our Lives*, turn it on, then sit in her wooden rocker beside the window.

Framed family photos fill every available space. A poster-sized shot above the TV stands out. In the center of a large group, Mabel and Willy hold the "Tango" painting that now hangs over their bed. Their fiftieth wedding anniversary.

I sigh and look away. The sky outside is grey and all around the oak leaves are turning from gold to rust. Many have already crinkled and fallen, while others hang tenuously on their branches as the wind teases at them.

Morley comes into the room with the tired-looking nurse who wheeled Mabel away when Willy didn't recognize her.

"How's our Mabel doing?" She leans over and speaks loudly to Mabel, who shifts to the side, intent on the television screen. The nurse puts the little paper cup of pills on Mabel's tray table, shakes her head, rises and looks at me. "Mabel's so lucky to have her cousin here," she says, and I look at Morley behind her who nods his head with vigor.

I clear my throat. "Yes, we've been doing lots of catching up," I say as Morley quietly moves behind the nurse, inching toward Mabel.

"We're so short staffed these days, and there've been so many sick calls I'm all alone on this floor for the rest of the week." She shrugs her shoulders and turns back to Mabel. "I don't know how they expect us to do it all. It takes so much time to give some of these folks their meds."

No sooner are those words out of her mouth when I see Morley plunk his sizeable cowboy boot firmly on Mabel's little slippered foot. As Mabel wails and wiggles trying to free herself, Morley, whose foot is out of the nurse's line of sight, seems to increase pressure, leading to predictable, deafening results.

"I was afraid this might happen," Morley stays cool above the clamor. "Old Mabel had a thing about nurses, thought Willy flirted with them over the years, so she's never been fond of them getting close to her. Maybe let cousin Frances try to get those meds into her."

I grit my teeth in a phony smile, and my head quavers more than usual as I send daggers with my eyes over her shoulder to Morley who might get whiplash from all the nodding he's doing, or I might just inflict it on him when the nurse leaves.

"I'll try," I say and quickly bend over blocking the nurse's view, as Morley lifts his big clodhopper from Mabel's foot and she stops howling. With as much deftness as I can muster I slip the pills into the tissue I keep in my sweater sleeve, and lift a glass of water to Mabel's lips. She takes a gulp, and I turn to the nurse. "That was easy enough. I'll be here to help whenever she gets her meds."

"The med run is at eight in the morning and again at eight before bed. I'll let the other nurses know. You're a godsend, Frances, a real godsend."

I almost choke. "Oh, I wouldn't look at it that way."

As soon as the nurse is out of earshot, I turn on Morley. He raises both palms in the air. "Frances, you know I wouldn't really hurt Mabel. It looked worse than it was. I just needed to get her worked up a bit. And don't worry your little Catholic conscience. I'm the one who will commit the sin. You just be here. I'll flush the pills." He opens a palm, and I drop the pills from my tissue into it.

My shoulders sag. I look at him for a good minute, then out to the rusting leaves still clinging to their branches. I turn back to him. "Okay, boss. Let's get this plan in action."

It's only a week later and Morley, Mabel and I sit in our usual spots with our deck of cards at the dining table.

"I'm so glad you're back, Sleeping Beauty," Morley says to Mabel.

"It's so weird, you know? I can't remember anything. It's like a fog. Faces, the TV. Is that what a 'bad trip' was like back in the day, Morley?"

Morley coughs, glances at me then looks back to his cards.

"Well, Mabel, I only experimented with that junk a couple of times. Stupid kid stuff."

"You were hardly a kid," she frowns. "Gert was a saint to put up with your shenanigans as long as she did. Wacky tobacky was your specialty, right? And we all tried that." She looks at me. "Most of us, anyway. These drugs were different. A little weed might have helped me, but not this stuff. I can't thank you both enough for what you did." She tears up, reaches out and grabs both our hands. She sniffs. "It's going to be hard, damned hardest thing I've ever had to do. So I still need you. Please help me let go of Willy."

Morley grins at Mabel.

"What?" she asks.

"I'll help you, Mabel, darling. Do you trust me?"

She starts to grin herself, "With my life. You just saved it."

"Well, I have a plan."

I've heard this before. He's got my attention.

"I hear the doctor's away for a while," he says, and I feel stress drain from me.

"There's no time to lose," he continues. "Tomorrow, ladies, we start operation Free Willy."

"I knew you weren't just another pretty face," Morley says as he and Mabel read the computer screen over my shoulder. He is so close his humid breaths waft down over me, lift the little hairs on the back of my neck, and I have real trouble concentrating on the information in front of us. "Looks like you were right about the memory pill," he says.

"Yeah, thank God for St. Frances," Mabel adds, and I wince.

"Willy's legs and arms were stiff as frozen laundry. So brittle, every time I touched him, I was afraid something would break. He only stopped whimpering when I massaged him, and I did that for hours. Until you stopped the memory pill, Frances."

I straighten and push my stool back from the computer, out of range of Morley's spell. "Now look, you two. I didn't stop anything. And I'm not sure whether it was the memory pill or the others we cut back. I'm no physician. Morley, you asked me to figure out the side effects. I'm only…"

"Calm down, Frances," Mabel says. "I know these aren't your decisions, girl. I'm just grateful for your Ph.D. brain. You explain. I decide. I stop the meds. Of course, my partner in crime here helps me do it." She flicks her thumb like a hitchhiker in Morley's direction and bursts into a toothy grin. "Without you two I wouldn't be able to figure out what to do and I wouldn't be able to do what I figure out." The smile fades, her eyelids lower and she fixes a wistful gaze on a spot somewhere past me. "Truth be told, I was at the point of ending it all."

Her words wick the fire from my mood. I reach out to touch her but she waves me off. Her re-focused eyes lock on mine and charge me with new purpose. "C'mon, girl," she says. "I'm gettin' my Willy back. He's moving his arms and legs again. What's next?"

We turn back to the computer. "I'm afraid some of the meds gave him neuroleptic malignant syndrome."

"English please, Doctor," Morley says.

"His antipsychotic drug is otherwise known as a neuroleptic, and this is a pretty high dose for someone his age. Especially in combination with some of his other drugs. Can cause muscle rigidity."

"Strike one," Morley says.

"… confusion…"

"Strike two," he says.

"Sweating," I hold my hand up to stop him from saying anything else, "and other things. Morley, this is no game. This condition is life-threatening." Mabel flinches. "It's okay dear," I say to her. "The symptoms subsided since you cut the yellow pill in half and stopped the others. But we have to be careful with this antipsychotic and the antidepressant. I wasn't so nervous about stopping the others. But these are tricky. Why is he on them, anyway? Was he seeing things?"

"He thought he was hearing 'angels' from the neighbor's apartment. Whenever he told me that, I just put new batteries in his hearing aids. Then he'd curse because he'd realize the 'angel' music was just radio noise from next door. He never wanted me to go with him to the doctor, and last time he complained about the 'angels' to her, he came home with the pink pill to silence the 'angels.' I don't blame the doctor. I could've told her. But the stubborn old fool insisted on his damn privacy."

Privacy. So loosely handled in the medical world. Like my last emergency room visit. I recognized the businessman on the stretcher next to mine, even waved at him when he came in. A young resident breezed in behind him, told him to drop his drawers. Then he yanked the flimsy, cloth curtain shut between me and the salacious details that transmitted his sexual disease. I needed to be deaf not to hear. But Mabel can't listen in on Willy?

"And the antidepressant…was he despondent?" I ask.

Mabel shrugs her shoulders. "The home's doctor added the white pill and a couple more to everything our family doctor prescribed."

Morley grits his teeth. "Stupid bastards."

"From what I read, it would be best to gradually stop one, then the other. He gets the antipsychotic morning and night. Maybe stop the morning pill for a few days, keep an eye out for changes, then take away the night pill. When that's done, we can decrease the antidepressant." I spin my stool around to face Mabel again. "What do you think?"

She looks up at Morley, who is still snarling. "If it was up to me," he says, "I'd just stop it all. Now. Worked for me in my thirties."

Mabel grasps Morley's clenched fist and holds his gaze. "You were one strong, young bugger in those days. Willy's a weak, old man. I say we do it the way Frances suggests. I know Willy. I'll be able to tell if it's hurting or helping him and if we can speed up. Okay?"

Morley's eyes moisten before he pulls Mabel into a bear hug. "Gert finally taught me how smart women are. Of course, we'll do it your way, darling."

She slaps at him. "Leave me be, you old flirt." She actually blushes, and I can't believe the heat under my own collar. Jealous? Of that old lech?

Hard to believe, but it's only two weeks later when there are four of us at our regular table long after dinner has ended. Willy is a little taller than Mabel, gaunt looking, bald and starving. If his natural state is plump, as Morley described, he has a job ahead of him. And he's well on his way, eating three helpings of lasagna at dinner and now getting himself an ice cream cone in the residents' kitchenette off the dining room.

"This is how it started," Mabel says and heads toward him. "Honey, the ice cream goes in the freezer, not the cupboard." She removes the brick of chocolate chunk from the cupboard above the sink and trades it with the cones he'd put in the freezer.

Willy hangs his head. "Don't know how I do such stupid things."

"Hey bud, if that's the worst you do, you could run the government," Morley says. "They're always misplacing way more important stuff, mainly money, and lots of it."

Willy chuckles as he sits down. "They still doing that stuff?"

Morley nods, pulls out his smartphone, and scans the Internet, showing Willy some news he missed.

"Good to know not much changed when I was out of it," Willy says. "I've learned my lesson. I'm never talking to another doctor without my Mabel with me." He pauses. "If I remember."

"Speaking of doctors, what's he saying about your newfound mobility?" Morley asks.

"He just got back this morning. When he saw Willy walking he looked stunned. Said it was a miracle," Mabel answers.

"Good," Morley says. "He hasn't figured it out."

Mabel puts one hand on mine, her other on Morley's. "The real miracle was meeting you two in here. If there's ever anything we can do for you, please, don't hesitate."

"Just make good use of that double bed you have," Morley laughs. "I can live vicariously through you kids."

Willy snorts. "Don't worry. I haven't forgotten what that's for."

"Men," Mabel says. "Do you never live long enough to get sex off your minds?"

"Mabel dear, the flesh may get weak, but as far as I can tell, the mind will always be willing," Morley answers.

Morley's phone buzzes again just as Jenny at the nursing station flicks the light switch. She glances about, as though checking whether the coast is clear, then beckons for Morley to join her. She huddles him close and starts to talk. They're too far away for us to hear anything, but Morley steps back, like someone surprised. After that, Jenny shakes her head and extends her arms in apparent frustration, as he mostly listens. They carry on for about five minutes. Finally, the two appear to nod in some kind of agreement before Morley saunters back to us and sits down.

"What was that about?" Mabel asks.

"They figured out what we did." His face is unreadable.

My stomach flutters and my hand vibrates at twice its usual speed. "My God. Who knows?"

"Sounds like only the night staff so far," Morley says in a somber tone.

"What should we do?" Now my stomach churns, and I instantly add police uniforms to the white coats I imagine might take me away.

"Apparently, the doctor's off somewhere again. This time for a month," he says and my hand slows down. "We have a plan." He looks to be fighting a grin.

Mabel smiles. "So, my friend, what's the plan?"

"Have you met Margie in Starlight Wing?" he asks.

We shake our heads.

"You will," he says. "No time to lose. Tomorrow we start operation Free Margie."

Only a month after we freed Margie, a chunky, seventy-something, Irish woman with bright eyes and a broad smile, we are eighteen liberated patients. The number is sure to increase, especially since we've discovered a retired pharmacist, a chemistry professor, and two nurses in our midst. But night staff report that not everyone on dayshift is happy with the surge in activity, complaining that more mobile patients add to their work. We need to figure out how to stay free without drawing attention. We gather in the dining room at eleven o'clock while the rest of the residents sleep. Two workers stand sentry nearby. People chat, laugh, and walk about like they did when I first moved in. Margie stretches over her walker and uses a fork to tap a glass on the table in front of her. Mabel stands beside her.

"We asked you all here because we have a plan," Mabel says.

"Whatever it is, you have my support," a large man calls out from the back. "You got us this far."

Everyone claps.

"We don't want to get staff in trouble. With only one worker on this wing after eleven, that's when we can have freedom. We're hoping you'll all agree to live a little at night, sleep during the day."

"Reverse our day?" a slight woman in a wheelchair asks.

"Exactly," Morley says. "Nighttime is party time. Staff will ignore us. We can have fun. No one else will know. No one gets in trouble. I know a bunch of you have these things." He holds up his phone. "We can use 'em to text each other, communicate quietly."

"I have a couple of extra phones," Rajeev, the distinguished-looking Indian gentleman, says. "If anyone wants to leap into the new world with us, I'm happy to give lessons."

"When's the party start?" one fellow asks.

"No time like the present," Morley says. "Colbert's on in the TV room, poker in the dining room."

"We'll get some music for Saturday night," Mabel adds. "Thought we'd do some dancing."

"Right on," a little octogenarian at a front table springs to her feet, wiggles her hips and everyone applauds. The group disperses with at least a third of them heads bent, texting on their devices. Am I the only one worried about how to keep this quiet?

The four of us are sitting together at our sixth Saturday night dance. All the residents on Sunshine Wing are in on the conspiracy now and the entire night shift is helping us. They even brought in a sound system. The dining-room-turned-dance-floor has been pulsating for an hour and I should be having the same fun as everyone, but something is wrong. I just know it.

I look to Morley, Mabel, then Willy, but each averts my eyes, just as they have for days. "How can day shift not notice all the texting?" I ask.

"Everyone's careful," Mabel says. "We're only messaging in our rooms. Besides, it's not all texting, people play games on their phones."

I don't like the way she looks down and squeezes Willy's hand.

"Some staff know. Others don't care. They're just happy we're all sleeping so much during the day. And the nimrod doctor just thinks it's normal for his patients to be comatose," Morley says.

Call me paranoid, but I'm not buying any of it. "Who is everyone talking to on those irritating little contraptions? And all the pictures everyone took at our dance last week. I know it was a masquerade and we all had masks on but aren't you worried someone will send this stuff to the outside world?" The quick look Morley and Mabel exchange does nothing to calm my fears. "What aren't you telling me?" I ask, just as the hip-wiggling, little octogenarian jumps up from the adjacent table.

"Play our anthem. Let's rock this joint," she calls to the DJ.

In seconds Neil Young is singing, "Rockin' in the Free World." Morley tugs at my hand. "They're playing our song," he grins.

Really? "Our song?" The nerve of the old coot. The lines keep on coming. Just like my husband, in the beginning. Empty words.

He pulls at me again. What the hell. I'm not getting anywhere with these questions, and I like to dance. Who cares whose song it is? I let him take me.

Three women gyrate, their perfumes mingle together in a dense scent that hangs in the air. One man moves his wife back and forth in a wheelchair and I catch a whiff of Old Spice as Mabel and Willy, who tango to every tune no matter what the beat, slide past us, cheek to cheek.

When the music stops, I'm spent. I follow Morley to our seats as Mabel steers Willy back to our table from the closet he's walked into. She leans toward us and raises her voice above Bill Haley's, "Rockin' Round the Clock."

"I think they're just about ready," she winks at Morley and Willy, and now I'm really irritated.

"Who's ready, and for what?" I ask through gritted teeth.

"It's a surprise," Willy says, and I soften. Who could be mad at such a sweet soul? I raise my eyebrows, and Willy continues. "You have a birthday tomorrow don't you, Frances?"

I widen my eyes. "How did you know that?"

Willy grins and nods in the direction of Morley who looks altogether too pleased with himself.

The music stops and the DJ announces, "Okay everyone, we're ready. Into the TV room." He gestures to me, "After you, birthday girl."

About three dozen of us gather around Rajeev standing beside the fifty-inch smart TV. The screen is paused on a YouTube page with the message, "Dedicated to St. Frances. Happy Birthday from PETS!"

"What's this?" I ask.

"It's our way of thanking you, Frances," Willy says.

"But I don't understand."

"It's spreading," Mabel says.

"What's spreading?"

She gestures at the people around the room. "Our movement."

Movement?

"You were right. We've been sending messages."

I knew it. My nails tap double time on the table beside me as my tremor speeds up. What kind of trouble are we in?

"We've shared what's happened here with relatives and friends across Canada, Britain, Australia, Europe, the States, Japan. Rajeev even sent word to India." As Mabel says this, Rajeev clasps his hands in prayer fashion and bows toward me.

I stare at the static screen. "PETS?" I ask.

"It's a new organization," Margie says from across the room. "Stands for People for the Ethical Treatment of Seniors. Members have been dressing up in elder masks and costumes and picketing government buildings in capitals around the globe. We have a Facebook page."

"It's okay, Frances," Mabel says when I shudder. "Everyone is keeping names confidential. It's the concept that's spreading. Mr. Gravel over there," she points to a short man with a silver goatee, "said it's just like the French resistance in World War II. They sent encrypted radio messages. Facebook is our underground network. It's happening everywhere. Old folks in homes quietly helping each other get off drugs, coming alive at night. In some places, doctors and nurses are leading the efforts."

I can't believe what I'm hearing. "How widespread is this?"

"See for yourself," Rajeev presses "play" on the YouTube video.

Unbelievable. There we all are, masked, dancing to the Beatles's "Revolution," but only for a brief moment. The scene shifts from one masked group of old folks to another with varying clothing styles, skin tones, all bopping in different settings.

"It went viral overnight," Margie says. "Now there's even talk of mass, synchronized flash mobs around the world."

"Look what you started, Frances," Morley says.

I shake my shaky head. "Me? No, no. This isn't my fault." He's laying it all on me. I should've known.

"No," Mabel says, "your accomplishment, Frances." She salutes me and the group applauds.

I stand agape as person after person hugs me on the way to the dance floor.

Mabel is last to embrace me before turning to Willy. "C'mon honey, this is *our* song." She winks at Morley and pulls Willy toward three other couples cuddling to Nat King Cole's, "Unforgettable." Willy and Mabel press cheeks together, strike a tango pose and glide away.

Morley laughs, turns back, looks intently at me.

"Frances, we need to talk."

"So, talk," I answer.

"Alone." He grasps my hand, leads me back to my room, closes the door.

"Frances," his voice is husky, "about the doctor."

I flinch.

"You're not alone anymore. I'll fend him off, and anyone else who gives you grief."

I feel like that thirteen-year-old again, all jittery inside.

"We need to take this relationship to the next level."

He pulls me toward him, loosens my hair, kisses my neck. I shiver. He must interpret that as consent, because he opens the button at my throat.

No, no. He does this with every girl, I think, and just then catch a glimpse of the outer me in the mirror. *Girl.* Ha. Hardly. Once again, I glare at myself. *Time's wasting, Frances.*

"But I'm. . . I..shake...and...I..."

He puts his finger to my lips. "Sshhh... Frances, darling, do you trust me?"

My heart thuds in my chest. The image of a hummingbird flits through my mind.

"With my life," I whisper. "What's left of it."

"I have a plan." He grins down at me, that heart-melting, boyish grin of his.

"Okay, boss, let's get this plan in action."

"No time to lose, darling. Operation Free Frances starts now."

ACKNOWLEDGEMENTS

Deep gratitude to Kathryn Trueblood for pulling *Awake* out of Minerva Rising's slush pile; to Kim Brown for the dedication, determination and infectious enthusiasm she demonstrates in showcasing women's stories; and to her Minerva Rising team members, Alissa DeLaFuente and Rebecca Beardsall, for their grace and care in guiding *Awake* out to the world.

Thank you to my dear sister/friend Brenda Longfellow for the photo and for suggesting, when I first poked my head out of the fiction writing closet many years ago, "Take some courses." That gentle nudge led me to writing teacher extraordinaire, Barbara Rogan. I will be forever grateful for her tutelage during two on-line classes, and for the feedback and encouragement from the women (and two men) I met there. A particular blessing from those sessions was the ensuing friendship with Pamela O'Flynn-Augusto, who lured me to my first (and only) writing conference in San Francisco, then onward to the magic of Maui. It was during my mother's harrowing journey through the healthcare system that Barbara, Pam and the others in those courses helped me learn the craft and give birth to *Awake* and other stories.

Along the way I felt the solitude of writing life, and often wondered the point of it all, but was unable to stop myself. So, it was with actual joy when my friend and colleague Erna Bujna seemed to really enjoy my work. My first willing reader. Her encouragement fueled my resolve to keep on keepin' on. Big thanks to beta readers Frances Jackson and Jean Kuehl for taking me across the finish line on this and other stories, and for kindred swimming spirit Kim Fahner for modeling a writing life.

Awake and other stories about healthcare wouldn't have happened without the much appreciated help of family and friends during my mom's difficult journey through a challenging system. Deep love and gratitude to my aunts (in alphabetical order) Bernice, Helena, Jeanette, Marg and Trish for being there physically and emotionally for us, and to uncles Gus, Mic and Randy for their solid support. And for sister-in-law Nancy for her on-going attention to my mom.

It helped in those days to find quiet oases of calm and understanding in chosen sisters Pauline Dietrich, Paula Walsh, Sandy Niemelainen, Sally (and Ken) Miller, Dale Canapini and Kirsti Hirvi who together with my blood relatives remind me of the Agatha Christie quote, "Family is a life jacket in the stormy sea of life."

While *Awake* spotlights one of the challenges in healthcare, I would be remiss not to acknowledge the daily small and large acts of kindness I witnessed from healthcare angels in the form of personal support workers, nurses, doctors, ambulance, dietary, cleaning, laboratory, respiratory, activity, pharmacy and others.

And of course, eternal love and thanks to my two guys. To Larry, my muse, for his always unvarnished truth and inimitable quick wit. And to Vance, my gently constructive critic, and ever my highest inspiration.

ABOUT THE AUTHOR

Nancy Johnson lives with her life partner on a lake in the Canadian Shield, about 200 miles north of Toronto, Canada. For over a decade, she has volunteered with family councils advocating for life, not just existence for their loved ones in long-term care. Nancy has been writing fiction forever but since retiring from full-time work in 2019, has made a greater effort to share her stories. *Awake* is Nancy's first publication by a fiction press. She just completed a novel about the same cast of characters set during COVID-19 and has resumed work on a manuscript inspired by her Newfoundland roots.

www.ingramcontent.com/pod-product-compliance
Lightning Source LLC
LaVergne TN
LVHW050947080826
845145LV00004B/1448

* 9 7 8 1 9 5 0 8 1 1 1 2 0 *